MW01170685

The RAINBOW of HOPE

Anita Eubank

Illustrated by

Gary Politzer

ISBN 0-9740022-6-7
Library of Congress Number 2003092875

First Edition

Author
Anita Eubank

Illustrator
Gary Politzer

Book Design
Deanne Delbridge

Cover Design
Amy Fritz

Co-Design / Production
Audrey Gordon

Author's Photograph
Lois Tema

The Rainbow of Hope may be ordered directly from:

The Rainbow of Hope Press
P.O. Box 472
Sausalito, CA 94966-0472

www.therainbowofhope.net

info@therainbowofhope.net

amazon.com

Printed in China

I dedicate this book of God's words to Master Zhi Gang Sha,
to the children of future generations, and to the child within each one of us
who would seek to know God.

Foreword

Millions of people search for soul wisdom and knowledge. More and more individuals pay great attention to their spiritual journey. They want to transform their lives, and reach enlightenment.

The Rainbow of Hope is a heart touching story about how a soul can find Love and Light. The process of the lost soul in search of the Light reflects the process from dark to light in so many people's spiritual journey. This story offers profound teaching. It gives the highest essence of the secret to personal transformation and the key to soul enlightenment. The essence is Love and Light.

This book is for everyone from children to elders. The wisdom within it explains that everyone can open their hearts and minds to directly receive the Love and the Light of God, which is within everyone and everything, every moment.

I am inspired and have personally benefited from *The Rainbow of Hope*. I'm confident that you will receive blessings from this enlightened teaching. *The Rainbow of Hope* is a direct message and priceless gift from God received through the open spiritual channel of Anita Eubank. This Love and Light will stay with you forever. May the teaching of this book serve you well.

God's blessing for everyone.

Zhi Gang Sha
San Francisco, California 2003

The RAINBOW of HOPE

*O*ut of the hills
and into the night

there came...

One Beloved Soul.

And the Soul said, "Where,
where do I find the *L*ight?"

"Where… where… **Where?**"

And *We* couldn't answer.

Now, as the Soul
continued,

walking, journeying,
            traveling far...

The soul felt hungry
    but couldn't eat.

The soul felt thirsty
    but couldn't drink.

"Where, where, where
    do I find food and drink?"

"Where is my sustenance?
    How can I find my nurturance?"
the Soul wondered,
    questioned, asked.

"How can I feed myself?
I have no hands."

The Soul looked down
    and said, "I have no feet.
I have no hands or feet!"

"How can I feed myself?
How can I drink?"

*A*nd so the Soul
wandered further
in search of an answer
to the most **fundamental
question...**

"How will I survive?"

"How can I survive?
How can I survive
    when I have no means
    of support?"

"I have no way
no way
to care for myself
to nurture myself
to clothe myself
to feed myself."

"I have no way to meet
my basic needs,
my most **fundamental needs
of existence!**"

"How can I $\mathcal{L}$ive?"

So the Soul went on further
   in the search of life,

"How can I live
   when I have no hands,
and no feet?"

"I have no eyes!"

"How can I see?
   I cannot see.
      I cannot see!"

"Where is the *Light*?"

"I am in the dark
        and there is no light,
no light.
        I am totally blind."

"I cannot reach for the stars.
        I know not where they are.
I have no reference point,
        no way to guide myself.
I have no means to find my way."

"I am alone,
alone in the Dark!"

The Soul paused
        and felt for a pulse.
"Uh! I have no heart.
        I have no pulse.
That means I have no heart!"

"How can I live when I have no heart?
        I have no heart.
That means I cannot love.
        How can I love when I have no heart?"

Indeed, this was a problem.

The Soul could not *Give*
or *Receive*
without a heart!

"Well, at least I have a mouth.
I can cry out."

But when the Soul would speak,
he discovered
he had no lips.

"I have no lips!
How could I have a mouth
without lips?"

This was indeed a puzzle.

So, the Soul went in search
     of a mirror
so he might see his face
     and discover
how it could be
     he had no lips.

Well, this became an increasingly
     difficult problem.

So, inwardly, he began to cry,
     and cry, and **cry.**

And with his crying,
      great salty tears
flowed from the holes
      that would have been
his eyes.

And the poor lonely Soul
        cried, and cried, and cried
until he could cry no more...

…but discovered
   that he was sitting in an ocean
of his own tears.

And he began to **float.**

"I'm floating! I'm floating!"
cried the Soul.

"What a wonder this is.
I can float!"

And within the floating
    came a small, delicate tone.

"Now, what could that be,
    that **amazing tone?**"

Behold, the Soul could hear
the sound of laughter.

"What? I hear laughter!
My, what a beautiful sound

Laughter."

"How remarkable.
I hear the sound
of **two people laughing.**"

"*I* am not alone!"

cried the Soul.

"I am floating,
        and I can hear the sound
of two people laughing."

"Whoah! What a **Joyful Note**!
        What a joyful note that sounds."

And so,
        floating in a puddle
                of his own tears,
                        the Soul began to $\mathcal{S}$ing.

And he sang,
     and he sang,
and he sang,

a *J*oyful Song.

And as he sang, he heard a ringing.

"Now, what could be the source
     of that ringing?" wondered the Soul.

"Well," said a voice,
    "Come and see."

"Whoah!" said the Soul,
    "I heard a voice,
and the voice invited me
    to look and see."

So the little Soul
        began bobbing along
in his salty ocean,

and discovered...

the most *B*eautiful Maiden

he ever did see!

And **what could she have been doing?**

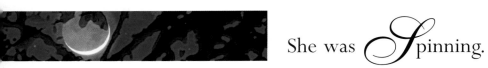 She was *Spinning*.

She was spinning a Golden Thread of Light.

"Whoah!" said the Soul,
    "That's truly, truly beautiful!

How did you learn to **spin gold?**"
    wondered the Soul.

"Well," said the Maiden,

"I learned it from God."

"You learned it from God?"
        asked the Soul.

"Yes!" said the Maiden.

"I learned how to Laugh.
        Then I learned how to Sing.

And then I began Spinning Gold!"

"Whoah!" said the Soul,
     "Could I hold the Thread?"

And he took the Golden Thread
in his... **Hand!**

"Uh!" said the Soul,
      "I've got a hand. Look!

And **I'm holding a** *Golden* **Thread.**"

"What would happen
      if I pulled on this thread?"

"Well," said the Maiden.
      "Try it and see."

So the Soul began
pulling and pulling
on the Golden Thread,
        and found he was climbing
higher and higher
        and lifting himself out
of the salty water.

And higher and higher did he climb
on the Golden Thread.
        And further and further
he lifted himself out of the salty water
        until he could… **See!**

And he saw a $\mathcal{R}$ainbow!

"Behold! It is a magnificently beautiful,
    shining bright light of many, many hues.
It's the loveliest thing I've ever seen."

"What a magnificent thing is a *Rainbow!*"

And he knew that a Rainbow occurs
when sunlight shines through water.

And he knew that his **tears**
had helped to make the Rainbow.

And so, he knew
he had done a *G*ood thing!

And he **Smiled!**
And his smile shone back at him
in Radiant Light.

And he began to **Feel!**

And he said, "Whoah!
    If I can feel,
that means I have a **Heart.**"

"And if I have a heart,
    could that mean I can **Love?**"

And with that, the Rainbow shone
    ever more, ever more brightly.
And the Soul said,

"I can *Love!*"

And with that, the Sun came out
and shone, and shone, and shone,
chasing all his doubt and fear away,
and the clouds that had covered
the Soul's Eyes.

And he said, "I can See! **I can See!**"

"I see the Light!"

And that is how the Soul found the $\mathcal{L}$ight,

and the *Love.*

and the *Rainbow* of *Hope.*

Author's Note

At the beginning of my spiritual journey, in my mid-twenties, I went to see a wise woman. It was the first counsel from a person with psychic abilities I had ever received. She said tersely, "You gonna' write a book!" As years passed, from time to time I wondered, "Where is the book? How am I to write it? What is it about?" I lived in anticipation that the book would make itself known to me. I waited and waited…

Fifteen years later, I attended a spiritual workshop in Italy. Suddenly, as I was standing talking to another woman, I felt a bolt of energy strike the base of my spine. The energy ricocheted to the ground as fast as lightening, turned around, travelled up my spinal column, and blasted out the top of my head with so much force it knocked me over.

Since that day in Italy, August 17, 1984, I have opened to a conscious relationship with the spiritual world. I was taught and healed by a force I called "the energy presence." Later, when I developed the capability of hearing words from spiritual consciousness, I came to know that this loving presence was Mary, "Mother Mary." She is my primary spirit guide, among many beloved guides. During that early intense healing process, which lasted for several years, I re-experienced situations where I knew tragedy in past lives, and was given the energy of pure love to heal my heart. I was also educated in the art of using the energy of love to heal others. This became the foundation for my ongoing healing and counseling work.

The year 2001 brought the fulfillment of the psychic's prophecy. I met a wise man leading a workshop on "How to Communicate with the Spiritual World," part of his teaching series on Soul Study. I knew I must study with him. His name is Master Zhi Gang Sha. He is a doctor of both Western and Eastern medicine, and master spiritual healer.

I made a private appointment to meet with Master Sha. I had barely stepped inside the door of his office when he spontaneously said, "You're going to write a book!" With surprise and pleasure I responded, "Yes." We began the process of his guiding me to receive my book.

During that period of time, a major world tragedy occurred. While the world watched in stunned disbelief, on September 11, 2001, two airplanes flew into the twin towers of the World Trade Center in New York City. Thousands of people lost their lives while others were helpless to save them. It was a time of great confusion and sadness. What was happening? Why did it happen? What was the message behind the incident? The message to everyone is that the world needs love, forgiveness, peace, and hope.

Two weeks later after my first appointment, and still no book, I met with Master Sha again. He stated strongly, "If God wanted you to have a book, God would just give you a book. So, why don't you talk directly to God and say, 'God, would you please let the book flow out?'"

I followed his instructions and began to experience conversations with God. On the morning of September 21, 2001, I bowed my head in prayer saying, "I absolutely know that the book is your voice, your words, your heart." God responded, "In answer to your prayer, *WE* will give you the book."

The following morning, I prepared to record my daily conversation with God. But in place of my normal speech there suddenly came a musical sing-song voice which told, with increasing drama, a spiraling poetic parable. It was the story of a beloved soul who came to earth and after feeling lost and alone, finally found the *Light* and the *Love* and the *Rainbow of Hope. It was the Book!*

The flow of God's voice through my open spiritual channel lasted twenty minutes. After it was finished, tears of gratitude poured from my eyes. I had waited over thirty years for my book, and it was finally here!

I thanked God from the bottom of my heart, and God said, "This little book holds the key. We feel that all people must know the truth and power of our message. It is an instrument which will help children learn how to connect with God. We feel the inner child of everyone will be served."

I am delighted to offer the service of *The Rainbow of Hope* to you. Enjoy it and benefit from it. Thank you.

Anita Eubank
Sausalito, California   2003

Acknowledgments

I wish to thank my mother, Dorothy, for introducing me to the arts at an early age, and my father, Lowell, for guiding me with his gentle wisdom, and providing me with a strong foundation for all my life.

I am so grateful to Gary Politzer for bringing this spiritual message into visual form. Thank you for your great artistry.

I offer immeasurable thanks to Master Zhi Gang Sha for his inspired and practical guidance, and masterful Feng Shui wisdom.

I thank my remarkable book production team for their crystal vision and enthusiastic work: book designer, Deanne Delbridge, book cover designer, Amy Fritz, and design associate, Audrey Gordon; production manager, Alan Weisskopf; and editors, Andi Berrin, Lisa Alpine, and Diana Holland.

I deeply thank my treasured friends and family for their insightful suggestions along the way: Steven Donovan, Lynn McCann, my two sisters, Linda and Brenda, Barbara Yurchuck, Claire Garrison, Barbara Shere, Amayea Rae, Carolyn Braddock, Sheila O'Brien, and Gary's great friends; Alexandra Rossi, Sandra Dakota, Daniel Parsons, and Rob and Debra Glaeser.

And I warmly thank the outstanding individuals who have honored me and *The Rainbow of Hope* with their commentary: Angeles Arrien, Laura Huxley, Alan Jones, Hale Makua, Ashfaq Ishaq, Katriona Munthe-Lindgren, and Jack Canfield.

I thank you all from my heart. I love you.